MOBY SHINOBI

NINJA AT THE PET SHOP

by Luke Flowers

SCHOLASTIC INC.

FOR MY CUDDLY AND CARING NAOMI, AND HER FUZZY-FRIEND-LOVING HEART.

Library of Congress Cataloging-in-Publication Data

Names: Flowers, Luke, author, illustrator. | Flowers, Luke. Moby Shinobi; [3] | Title: Ninja at the pet shop / by Luke Flowers. | Other titles: Scholastic reader. Level 1. | Description: New York,: Scholastic Inc., 2018. | Series: Moby Shinobi; [3] | Series: Scholastic reader level 1 | Summary: Told in rhyme, Moby Shinobi tries to put his ninja skills to work helping out at the pet shop, but as usual his efforts result in complete chaos—until he redeems himself by finding the missing python. Identifiers: LCCN 2017022638| ISBN 9781338187267 (pbk.) | ISBN 9781338187274 (hardcover) Subjects: LCSH: Ninja—Juvenile fiction. | Helping behavior—Juvenile fiction. | Pet shops—Juvenile fiction. | Stories in rhyme. | Humorous stories. | CYAC: Stories in rhyme. | Ninja—Fiction. | Helpfulness—Fiction. | Pet shops—Fiction. | Humorous stories. | LCGFT: Stories in rhyme. Humorous fiction. | Classification: LCC PZ8.3.F672 Ne 2018 | DDC [E]—dc23 LC record available at https://lccn.loc.gov/2017022638

10 9 8 7 6 5 4 3 2 1   18 19 20 21 22

Printed in the U.S.A.   40
First printing 2018
Book design by Steve Ponzo

3

Look! Spin! Snag! I am ninja brave!

Jog! Leap! Reach! Ninjas love to save!

Hop! Pull! Stop! I am super strong!

4

8

Moby thinks of big twists and bounds!
He grabs a brush to wash the hounds.

13

Moby thinks of a ninja flip.
He opens a bag with a RIP.

Josh plays with each group one by one.
Other pets wait for playtime fun!

19

Moby thinks of his ninja gym.
Can ALL the pets keep up with him?

HOP!

JOG!

23

25

Then all the pets let out a HOWL!
Even the birds are feeling foul!

Do not fret. I know where to start!
I have the bravest ninja heart!

Moby thinks of a big cartwheel.
This ninja is as strong as steel!

29